Custardly Wart
Pirate 3rd Class

Alan MacDonald

illustrations by Mark Beech

BLOOMSBURY

First published in Great Britain in 2008 by Bloomsbury Publishing Plc
36 Soho Square, London, WID 3QY

Text copyright © Alan MacDonald 2008
Illustrations copyright © Mark Beech 2008

The moral rights of the author and illustrators have been asserted

A CIP catalogue record of this book is available from the British Library

ISBN 978 0 7475 9467 3

All papers used by Bloomsbury Publishing are natural, recyclable products made
from wood grown in well-managed forests. The manufacturing processes conform to
the environmental regulations of the country of origin.

Printed in Great Britain by Clays Ltd, St Ives Plc

1 3 5 7 9 10 8 6 4 2

www.bloomsbury.com

It's Behind You!

Foreword

by

Professor Frank Lee Barking (M. A. D. Phil)

Since the dawn of time members of the hapless Wart family have been dogged by disaster. From facing flesh-eating ogres to grappling with gladiators and being kidnapped by pirates, Warts have looked Death in the eye and lived to tell the tale. Now, thanks to years of painstaking research, and literally hours of daydreaming, I am proud to bring you the absolutely true and epic saga of . . .

The History of Warts

Chapter 1

Wanted: Schoolteecher

Dankmarsh School lay just outside the sleepy village of Biggin-on-Sea, though it wasn't really on sea at all. To tell the truth it wasn't even on a puddle. Not one of the children at Dankmarsh had ever set eyes on the sea. Their days were spent staring at the grim, grey walls of the school and the grim, grey face of Miss Scrubshaw their schoolmistress. Miss Scrubshaw wore a black dress buttoned to the neck, black lace-up boots and a bonnet that

1

looked like it was made of cast iron. She taught the children reading, writing and everything else, since she was the only teacher in the school. But recently she had come to the conclusion that looking after thirty orphans was far too much work for one person so she had placed an advert in the *Bleakby Post*.

Wanted: schoolteecher for spoilt, ungrateful children.
Must be able to teech reading, riting and speling.
Bed and board plus very small wage.
Apply in person (with references) to –
The Schoolmistress,
Dankmarsh School,
Biggin-on-Sea.

The advert had appeared in the newspaper six weeks running, but whether it was the spoilt children or the pitiful wage or just the name Dankmarsh that put people off, no one ever replied.

One dark, rainy night the children were all in bed and fast asleep. All, that is, except for Custardly Wart. Custardly, in Miss Scrubshaw's opinion, was a troublesome child. He was a small boy with dark untidy hair and large brown eyes that seemed to follow her about the room. Miss Scrubshaw thought of him as a watch that had been wound up too tightly. In class he fidgeted, idled and shuffled his feet. Once he had even dared to interrupt her by putting up his hand to ask a question.

On this particular night, Custardly was trying to get to sleep by listing the reasons why he couldn't.

1. He was cold as a very cold icicle.
2. He was hungry (as usual).
3. Dobbs had taken most of the blanket (children slept two to a bed to save on sheets).
4. He thought he could hear voices outside.

He lay still and listened. The wind moaned, the windowpanes rattled and the rain drummed on the roof. But above this came the low murmur of voices and footsteps drawing nearer.

Thump, thump, thump! Custardly almost jumped out of his skin. Someone was hammering on the front door as if they meant to break it down. He sat up in bed. No one ever visited Dankmarsh School and certainly not in the dead of night.

Summoning his courage, he slipped out of bed and crept down the shadowy corridor to the landing. Through the banisters he could see Miss Scrubshaw in her nightdress drawing back the heavy bolt of the door. Into the hall stepped the most curious man he'd ever set eyes on. He had a black beard that reached almost to his eyes. His red coat, patched at the elbows, hung almost to his long black boots. When he swept off his three-cornered hat to make a bow, it emptied a puddle of rainwater on to the floor.

'Your servant, ma'am!' he said in a deep, ringing voice. 'My name is Captain Cuttlefish but you may call me . . . Captain.'

A small man, round as a barrel, suddenly popped out from behind him, grinning and winking. He shook Miss Scrubshaw's hand as if he were trying to pump her for water. 'A pleasure to meet you, miss, a pleasure!'

'Ah! this is my . . . um, cousin, Mr Mate,' said the Captain. 'Do I have the pleasure of addressing the schoolmistress?'

'I am Miss Scrubshaw,' replied Miss Scrubshaw coldly.

'And pretty as a poop deck you are, ma'am,' said the Captain, bending to kiss her hand.

Miss Scrubshaw snatched it back quickly, blushing to her toes. No one had ever called her pretty as a poop deck before – though she wasn't entirely sure what a poop deck was.

The Captain produced a soggy ball of newspaper from his pocket and smoothed it out.

'Well then, ma'am, I'm sorry to call so late but I'm told you're on the lookout for a teacher.'

'Oh, the advert.' Miss Scrubshaw suddenly sounded much less frosty. 'You've come about the job?'

'That I have, ma'am.'

'That is it in a nutshell or a seashell or any kind of shell you care to name,' winked Mr Mate. 'The Captain here has come about the job.'

The Captain bent down and muttered darkly in his ear, 'Pipe down, Mr Mate, and leave the talking to me.'

Miss Scrubshaw invited the two men into her study. As soon as they had disappeared inside, Custardly hurried downstairs and put his ear to the door to listen.

Miss Scrubshaw pulled her shawl around her and sat at her desk, regarding her dripping visitors with curiosity. They were a strange-looking pair. The tall Captain was pacing around the room studying the pictures on the walls with interest. The ruddy-faced Mr Mate lounged in an armchair, puffing away at a long clay pipe.

Miss Scrubshaw coughed and fanned away the smoke with her hand. 'Perhaps we should start by taking a look at your references,' she said. 'I trust you have brought them?'

'Ah yes, the references,' said the Captain. His eyes

swivelled like billiard balls. 'Did I give 'em to you, Mr Mate?'

Mr Mate shook his head. 'Not me, Captain. References – is that a kind of biscuit?'

'References,' said Miss Scrubshaw. 'Surely your last school gave you a letter of recommendation?'

'Ah to be sure, the letter. Now, where did I leave that?' The Captain patted the pockets of his coat and began to empty the contents. He brought out a compass, a ship-in-a-bottle, a pack of cards, a leather purse, a dagger, a pair of pistols and a half-sucked humbug and laid them all on the desk.

'Do you always carry so many weapons?' asked Miss Scrubshaw.

'Ah well,' said the Captain. 'At my last school the children was a little unruly. When you want a little quiet, you'd be surprised how effective a loaded pistol can be.'

'And where was your last school?' asked Miss Scrubshaw suspiciously.

'Oh, north of here,' said the Captain, stroking his silky but rather soggy beard. A picture on the wall caught his eye and he crossed the room to study it more closely.

'Now, this is a pretty little thing you have here,' he said. 'How did you come by it, I wonder?' It was an old map drawn in an inky hand with pictures of mermaids, dolphins and sharks bobbing in the sea.

'That?' said Miss Scrubshaw. 'It belonged to my Uncle Jack. He was a seafaring man. When he died, I inherited some of his things.'

'Uncle Jack, you say?' The Captain's eyes gleamed with interest. 'Was he a big man your uncle, with wild black hair, an eyepatch and a pet monkey called Mipps?'

'Yes. Why? Did you know him?'

'No, no,' said the Captain. 'It was just a wild guess.'

Mr Mate had come over to examine the map himself and excitedly seized the Captain by the arm. 'Captain!' he hissed.

'Not now, Mr Mate,' said the Captain, shooting him a warning look.

'But Captain, isn't that the . . . ARGHH!' The mate hopped around holding his foot, which the Captain seemed to have trodden on by accident.

The Captain settled himself in an armchair and rubbed his hands together.

'Well then, ma'am, as to them references, I'm sure they'll turn up by and by. But in the meantime what do you say? You need a teacher and I need a job.'

Miss Scrubshaw pursed her lips. 'Perhaps we should first discuss the matter of wages.'

The Captain leaned forward. 'Ah, wages. I like your thinking. What did you have in mind?'

'One shilling a month,' said Miss Scrubshaw.

The Captain's face fell. 'As low as that?'

'Less the rent for the room and the cost of your meals.'

'Meals. Of course,' said the Captain.

'Which comes to ten pence ha'penny a month. Leaving you a total of, let me see, a penny ha'penny a month.'

The Captain's face darkened. For a moment it seemed he might draw his cutlass, but instead he reached out a hand.

'Very generous, ma'am,' he smiled. 'I accept your terms.'

'Good. Lessons will start tomorrow at eight o'clock prompt,' said the schoolmistress.

'Isn't that a mite early?' asked the Captain. 'I don't usually rise before noon.'

'Breakfast at seven, lessons at eight. At Dankmarsh we believe in the three Ds – discipline, dullness and duty. Teaching is a battleground, Captain, and the children are the enemy. I do not hold with mollycoddling.'

'No indeed. 'Tis the worst thing, especially if your name is Molly,' agreed the Captain. He pocketed his belongings and turned to go.

'One thing more,' said the schoolmistress sharply.

'Yes, ma'am?'

'I would like my uncle's map back if it's not too much trouble.'

The Captain felt in his coat pocket and seemed shocked to discover that the map had somehow slipped in there, along with his other belongings. He handed it back with many humble apologies. Bowing low, he turned, opened the door and stepped into the hall, where he fell over Custardly Wart, who was crouched outside listening.

Miss Scrubshaw looked up. 'Good heavens! Is someone there?'

'Oh no, no one at all!' said the Captain. 'Must have been the cat got under my feet. Well good evening to you, ma'am, good evening!'

As Custardly dashed up the stairs, he glanced back and saw the Captain standing in the hallway, watching him thoughtfully.

Chapter 2

Lubber Lessons

The next morning the classroom door banged open. Much to the surprise of everyone except Custardly, in marched the Captain with Mr Mate bobbing along behind like a tugboat. He sat down at the teacher's desk and rested his great black boots on top of it. A frown crossed his face. He had overslept that morning and dressed in such a hurry he was still wearing his pyjama trousers (the black ones with the skull and crossbones).

He took out his dagger and started to slowly peel an apple. The children watched him hungrily. So did Mr Mate, who had missed breakfast and could hear his tummy rumbling like an outboard motor. The Captain cast an eye over his new class and scowled.

'Mr Mate,' he barked, 'what is the first rule of the sea?'

'Don't fall overboard,' said Mr Mate.

'No . . .' said the Captain.

'Always wear a hat when you're lying in the sun.'

'No,' snapped the Captain. 'The first rule.'

'Never spit into the wind,' suggested Mr Mate. 'Never set sail without biscuits. Never try to stroke a shark –'

'Pipe down, you fool!' thundered the Captain. 'The first rule of the sea is: "Never let your crew be idle." An idle crew is a crew that gets up to mischief. So why are these lubbers idle?'

Mr Mate rubbed his chin. 'Because they are waiting for orders?'

'Exactly, Mr Mate. And who gives the orders around here?'

'Beg'n pardon, Captain, you do.'

13

'I do because I am the Captain, and don't let any of you forget it.'

He surveyed the rows of pale children shivering in the draughty classroom. None of them uttered a word, mainly because they were too frightened to speak. They had never met a teacher armed with a dagger and cutlass before.

'You, boy!' The Captain pointed a finger at Custardly in the front row. 'What's your name?'

'Custardly, sir.'

'Custardly? You sound like a pudding! What do you do on a Monday morning, boy?'

'Please, sir, Miss Scrubshaw makes us copy out our letters,' replied Custardly Wart.

'Copy out letters? Suffering catfish!' cried the Captain. 'And you waste your time on this kind of hogwash every day?'

'Yes, sir,' said Custardly.

'Then when do you go outside?'

'Please, Miss Scrubshaw doesn't allow us outside.'

'She says fresh air is bad for children,' added Dobbs. 'We might catch a chill.'

The Captain put down his apple and gaped at them. 'You never go out? Not even for a walk? When do you get to the sea?'

Custardly glanced at the others. 'I've never seen the sea, sir,' he said. 'None of us has.'

'Splice me sideways with a boathook!' the Captain burst out. 'You hear that, Mr Mate? Never seen the sea!'

Mr Mate shook his head. 'The poor mites. It's 'eartless, Captain, that's what it is.'

'It's worse than heartless,' stormed the Captain. 'It's . . . it's headless.'

Angela Summers raised her hand.

'Please, Captain, what's the sea like?'

'Like?' The Captain blew out his cheeks. 'Well, it's blue.'

Mr Mate rubbed his stubbled chin.

'More of a green, I'd say, Captain. A greeny blue or a bluey green.'

'Bilge!' scoffed the Captain. 'Any lubber knows the sea is blue.'

'What about that one we found on the ship's globe? That was called the Red Sea.'

'Maybe it was red with the blood of fools who argued with their captains,' replied the Captain darkly. 'In any case, the colour isn't the thing. When you are out on the sea with the breeze a-blowing, the waves a-waving and the ship rolling . . . Strike me, why are we talking about it when we could show them?'

Mr Mate took out his pipe. 'Beg'n pardon, Captain?'

'Show them a ship, you fool.'

Custardly raised his hand again. 'But we're not allowed out of school.'

'Never mind that, shipmate!' cried the Captain,

warming to his idea. 'If you can't go to the sea then the sea will come to you. Look lively, Mr Mate, and set this crew to work!'

For the next twenty minutes, the children ran up and downstairs as orders flew thick and fast.

'Fetch buckets!' cried the Captain. 'Soap and water, Mr Mate!'

'Aye aye, Captain. Soap and water.'

'And rope, Mr Mate. We'll be needing lots of rope.'

'You, shipmate!' The Captain caught Custardly by the arm. 'Know where you can lay your hands on a piece of sailcloth?'

Custardly shook his head. 'I don't think so. There's only the sheets on our beds.'

'Just the job, boy, sheets! Bring 'em down here.'

'All of them?'

'All of 'em.'

Custardly nodded. 'Yes, sir. I mean aye aye, Captain.' He thumped upstairs to fetch the sheets, hoping he wouldn't bump into Miss Scrubshaw on the way.

*

The dusty classroom was a hive of activity as the children learned how to scrub a deck, patch a sail and climb the rigging. These things, the Captain claimed, were important to their education and would come in handy in the future. He retired to his desk to put his feet up while they worked.

Eventually the last sheet was hoisted into place and the class stood back to admire what they'd done.

'It's a boat!' said Dobbs.

'Boat be blowed!' scoffed the Captain. 'That, me hearties, is a ship.'

The room had certainly changed out of recognition. What had once been a dark, dingy classroom now boasted a deck as clean as a bosun's whistle. Six wooden benches formed the ship while brooms and mops bristled like cannons on both sides. The faded classroom walls had been painted sky blue with flying fish jumping the clouds (Custardly's idea). Instead of cobwebs, rigging hung from the rafters. Best of all was the skull-and-crossbones flag painted on one of Miss Scrubshaw's best pillowcases.

The children were eager to climb aboard but the Captain held them back.

'One last thing, shipmates. She needs a name.'

'The Captain's right,' nodded Mr Mate. 'You can't have a ship without a name.'

'Let's call her *The Golden Hind*!' cried Dobbs, who had read a lot of books.

'*The Golden Mermaid*!' said Angela.

'No,' said the Captain. 'We'll call her *The Captain's Revenge*. Revenge because it sounds scurvy and wicked and Captain because I thought of it.'

'What about *The Mate's Revenge*?' suggested Mr Mate.

No one thought much of this, maybe because the Captain had drawn his dagger again and was looking as if he might use it.

As soon as they were all on board the Captain leapt on to a chair. 'All hands on deck! Weigh the anchor! Hoist the mainsail!' he bellowed. He was starting to enjoy himself. Children were far easier to command than pirates – they obeyed orders and didn't keep pestering him for ship's biscuits.

'Where to, Captain?' asked Mr Mate.

'To the sea, Mr Mate. Set sail for the sea!'

Custardly couldn't imagine how a ship made of mops and benches could reach the sea but a moment later he found out. Three members of the junior crew stood at the back of the ship armed with buckets of soapy water.

'On the count of three,' said the Captain. 'One, two, three!'

SPLOSH! Three buckets of soapy water hit the floor in a torrent. The water slopped and slooshed and foamed around the ship just like real waves. The children cheered and whooped. It might have all ended well if, at that moment, Miss Scrubshaw

hadn't opened the classroom door to check on the Captain's first lesson. She turned pale as she took in the pillowcase flag, the sail made of bed sheets and the soapy water rushing towards her in a brown river. She took a step forward, trod on a bar of soap and performed an impressive double somersault, landing on her back. All the children could see of her was a pair of black woollen stockings sticking up from a froth of petticoats and bloomers.

It was Custardly who laughed first. He couldn't

help it. Miss Scrubshaw looked like a beetle struggling on its back. Her bonnet had slipped over her
face and when she pushed it back her face was purple
with rage.

'CAPTAIN!' she thundered. 'A WORD WITH
YOU!'

Chapter 3

What Custardly Heard

T hat evening the children were sent to bed early
without any supper. They lay huddled beneath
their blankets, trying not to think about food.

'Anyway, I told you he was a pirate,' whispered
Custardly.

Dobbs shivered with cold. 'You may be right,' he
said. 'But the question is why is he here and what
does he want?'

'That's two questions,' said Custardly.

'What are you talking about?' This came from the other side of the curtain where the girls slept.

'Nothing! Go back to sleep!' Custardly called back.

A second later there was a creak of floorboards and a pad of feet as Angela and Rose appeared through the curtain, shivering in their nightdresses and wrapped together in a thin brown blanket.

'She can't sleep,' announced Angela.

'Neither can she,' said Rose. 'We're hungry.'

'And cold,' said Angela. 'What are you talking about?'

'I told you, nothing,' said Custardly. 'Go back to bed.'

The girls took no notice and wriggled their way in at the other end of the bed. Custardly sighed and went back to their conversation.

'Maybe they're planning to rob us,' he suggested.

'Who?' Angela wanted to know.

'The pirates, of course. That's what pirates do – they plunder your gold.'

'We don't have any gold,' Dobbs pointed out. 'You couldn't plunder a sausage in this school.'

'I love sausages,' said Rose.

'Sausages with gravy and mash,' said Angela.

'Roast beef and parsnips,' said Rose.

'Plum pudding with custard,' said Dobbs.

'STOP IT!' cried Custardly. This was always happening. The more they tried not to think about food the more they ended up thinking about it. Somewhere outside he heard voices. Slipping out of bed, he went to the window. On the balcony directly below sat two shadowy figures, talking in low voices.

'Look – it's them! The pirates!' hissed Custardly.

The others hurried over to the window to look.

'What are they doing?' whispered Dobbs.

'Talking.'

'Yes, but what about?'

'How should I know?' said Custardly.

The children watched the pirates for a while, their breath misting the windowpane. They seemed to be having a heated discussion about something.

'I wish we could hear what they're saying,' said Angela.

Custardly peered into the darkness. 'Maybe we can.'

'How?'

'Simple. One of us has to climb down.'

A few feet from the window a twisted ivy bush clung to the wall. Dobbs looked doubtful. 'It's a long way down. What if you fall?'

'ME?' said Custardly. 'Who says I'm going?'

'Well, it's your idea,' argued Dobbs.

'Don't look at me,' said Angela. 'I'm scared of heights.'

'Me too,' said Rose.

'And I'm allergic to ivy,' said Dobbs.

Custardly looked out of the window. Actually, it was a *very* long way down.

On the balcony below the Captain paced up and down. He had to think and he could never think properly when he was thirsty. It was lucky he'd brought along a good supply of grog.[1]

'It's the map, Mr Mate, or I'm a Frenchman,' he said. 'I told you we'd find it here.'

'How do you know for sure, Captain?' asked the mate.

'Didn't you hear what she said? She got it from her Uncle Jack.'

---

1 **Grog** – A mixture of rum and water.

'Yes, but I thought the map we're looking for belonged to Black Jack Mulligan.'

'So it is, you brainless barnacle! Mulligan was her Uncle Jack.'

'Oh, I see!' said Mr Mate. 'I never knew his first name was Uncle.'

The Captain rolled his eyes. Sometimes he wondered why he'd chosen Mr Mate as his first mate. It was probably because his name was Mate. He went on pacing the balcony.

'Try to think,' he said. 'It's simple enough. We know the schoolteacher has the map and we know that she knows that we know where it is.'

Mr Mate frowned. 'I'm not sure I follow, Captain.'

'Which part don't you follow?'

'The part where you said it was simple.'

The Captain took another swig of grog.

'What I'm saying is how the devil do we get our hands on the map when she keeps it locked in her study?'

Mr Mate took off his cap and scratched his head. His face brightened. 'I have it, Captain! We could make her walk the plank!'

'Smart thinking, Mr Mate,' said the Captain.

'Thank you, Captain.'

'Except the sea is miles away and we don't have a plank.'

'Garrrr! I'd forgotten that,' said Mr Mate and fell to smoking his pipe and thinking once again.

'No,' said the Captain. 'What we need is some way to catch the old boot off guard. And then, once we have the map, there is the other thing.'

Mr Mate looked puzzled. 'What other thing?'

The Captain lowered his voice. '*You know*, the thing I told you never to speak of.'

Mr Mate knitted his brows, trying to remember. 'Oh, *the children*!' he burst out.

The Captain cut him off, clapping a hand over his mouth. 'Quiet, you fool! I said never to speak of it. What if someone was listening? You'll give the whole game away.'

If either the Captain or his mate had happened to look up they would have seen that someone was indeed listening. Custardly Wart had climbed out of the top-floor window and was now clinging precariously to the ivy some ten feet above their heads. He didn't weigh much but the branch holding him wasn't very thick and he was worried it might give way at any moment. To make matters worse, he was only wearing a thin nightshirt so his legs were trembling like teacups on a tray.

Silence had fallen on the balcony below, where the two pirates were still trying to think of a cunning plan. Every now and then one of them would jump up excitedly, then shake his head and go back to thinking. At last the Captain stopped pacing up and down.

'Wait! I have it!' he said. 'Mr Mate, what am I famous for?'

Mr Mate chewed on his pipe. 'Ooh well, that's a hard one, Captain.'

The Captain glared. 'Come on! Think, man. What do people say about me?'

'That you eat all the biscuits,' said Mr Mate.

'No, you fool! That I'm a handsome devil. That I know the way to any woman's heart.'

'Funny,' said the mate. 'I don't remember anyone saying that at all.'

The Captain didn't get a chance to argue because at that moment there was a loud crack above their heads. The pirates looked up just as something came hurtling towards them faster than a speeding cannonball.

'Aaaarrgghhh!' yelled Custardly.

'Help!' cried the Captain as he tried to leap out of the way.

'Ooof!' gasped Mr Mate as Custardly landed on top of him, luckily breaking his fall.

For a few seconds there was an untidy struggle of arms and legs as the startled pirates tried to escape.

'Help! I'm being eaten by a jellyfish!' cried Mr Mate.

'Ouch!'

'Argh!'

When at last they calmed down they saw that the monster that had fallen on them was only a small boy with a ripped nightshirt, and leaves in his dark, straggly hair.

'YOU!' roared the Captain. 'Where the devil did you come from?'

'Um . . . I sort of fell,' stammered Custardly.

'He was snooping more like,' said Mr Mate. 'He has the look of a spy, Captain. His ears are too close together.'

The Captain leaned in close so that Custardly could smell rum on his breath. The point of his cutlass pricked Custardly's throat.

'You know what we do with spies, boy?'

'Feed them cake?' said Custardly hopefully.

'Tell him, Mr Mate.'

Mr Mate drew a feather from his pocket. 'We ties them to a chair and tickles their feet.'

Custardly looked from one face to another. 'Is that all? I thought you were pirates.'

The Captain narrowed his eyes. 'And who says we are?'

'Well, anyone can see that,' said Custardly. 'You dress like pirates and you talk like pirates. And you're holding a cutlass. Teachers don't have cutlasses.'

Mr Mate shook his head. 'I told you! I said we should have come in disguise.'

The Captain glared at him. 'I'm not putting on a frock for anyone,' he growled.

He wrapped a friendly arm round Custardly's shoulder.

'So, lad. You're smart – I can see that. Not much gets past you. You'd make a good pirate.'

'Would I?' said Custardly, who could quite see

himself in a feathered hat and a gold earring.

'I'm sure of it, but seeing as you're so clever, tell me what else you know.'

'Well,' said Custardly. 'I know there's something you want and I know it's got something to do with the map in Miss Scrubshaw's study.'

The two pirates exchanged worried looks. 'Go on, lad. What else?' said the Captain. 'Say you had an interest in a certain map, how would you lay your hands on it?'

Custardly considered this. He felt sure by now the pirates weren't going to cut his throat. He had also guessed that the map was no ordinary map. If the pirates had come all this way to find it, then it followed that it was a treasure map, which meant it was worth something.

'What would you give me if I helped you?' he asked.

The Captain dug in his pocket and brought out a shining coin. 'See that, shipmate? That's a gold doubloon. Help us to the map and it's yours.'

Custardly's eyes shone. With that much money, he could buy bread and cheese, maybe even a plum pudding.

'You'd have to be clever,' he said. 'Miss Scrubshaw
goes to bed at ten o'clock every night and she always
locks the door of her study.'

'And what does she do before going to bed?' asked
the Captain.

'Nothing much,' said Custardly. 'She comes round
with a candle to make sure we're all asleep. Sometimes she sits in her room and darns her stockings or
counts her money. Once I saw her playing cards all
by herself.'

'Clap me in irons!' the Captain burst out. 'That's
it!'

'What?' asked Custardly.

Mr Mate suddenly tugged at the Captain's sleeve,
his eyes wide and his mouth opening and closing
like a fish.

The Captain clapped Custardly on the back. 'Never you mind, shipmate. Off you go and leave the rest to me. You've been a great help.'

'But Captain . . . !' cried the mate, pointing at the sky.

'What is it now, Mr Mate?'

The Captain finally turned and looked up. His eyes bulged with fear and he backed away towards the door of his room.

'Run!' he spluttered. 'Abandon ship! Women and captains first!'

'Aye aye, Captain!' cried Mr Mate.

The two pirates dived headfirst into their room, slamming the doors behind them and pulling the curtains. Custardly was left alone on the balcony, wondering what had caused the panic. Looking up, he saw a bat no bigger than a mouse swoop overhead and flap off into the starry night sky. The Captain and his mate peeped out from behind their curtains. Custardly shook his head. For a pair of black-hearted pirates they were certainly easily scared. And they hadn't even given him the money they'd promised.

Chapter 4

A Game of Knaves

The clock in the hall struck eleven. Custardly, who had been counting the bongs, sat up in bed and listened. He shook Dobbs by the shoulder.

'Dobbs! Are you awake?'

'No,' murmured Dobbs.

'Listen! I can hear something,' hissed Custardly.

'So can I,' grumbled Dobbs. 'It's you keeping me awake.'

'No. They're up to something downstairs. Listen!'

Dobbs rolled over and rubbed his eyes. Reaching for his glasses, he settled them on his nose. He could hear talking in the dining room below. A shrill laugh sounded remarkably like Miss Scrubshaw. But that was impossible – Miss Scrubshaw never laughed.

'I'm going to see what they're doing,' said Custardly, pushing back the blankets.

Dobbs stared at him. 'You're mad. What if she catches you?' he said.

'She won't,' replied Custardly. 'Are you coming or not?'

'No,' said Dobbs. 'Definitely and absolutely not.'

A minute later the two boys were padding bare-foot down the hallway in their nightshirts. As they reached the landing they dropped down on all fours and crawled forward until they could peer through the banisters at the room below.

Miss Scrubshaw was seated at the dining table with Mr Mate and the Captain, who was expertly shuffling a deck of cards. A bottle and glasses stood on the table, along with a piles of coins in front of each player. The schoolmistress's eyes shone in the firelight and for once she wasn't wearing her iron bonnet. She almost looked as if she was enjoying herself.

'So what's it to be, Miss Scrubshaw?' asked the Captain, riffling the cards. 'Snap? Old Maid? Schooner? Five Card Hokum? Muggins?

Miss Scrubshaw sipped her grog. She had never heard of these games – perhaps because the Captain had invented most of them.

'I'm afraid,' she said, 'I know very little about cards.'

'Come now, Miss Scrubshaw. No need to be modest,' said the Captain.

'Please, Captain, call me Constance.'

'And a pretty name it is too,' winked the Captain.

Mr Mate pushed his head between them. 'You can call me Eli if you like,' he offered.

'Pass the grog,' replied the Captain sharply. 'Care for another glass, Constance?'

'I really shouldn't,' said Miss Scrubshaw as her glass was refilled. 'I'm feeling quite light-headed. Are you sure this is a cordial?'

'Grog? 'Tis just something to keep the cold out. Much like a fruit punch, ain't that right, Mr Mate?' said the Captain.

'Aye, Captain, except with more of a punch,' winked the mate.

The Captain began to deal the cards at a dizzying speed. 'What do you say to a game of Knaves, Constance?' he suggested.

'I'm afraid I've never heard of it,' said Miss Scrubshaw. 'Is it easy to pick up?'

The Captain replied that it was as easy as falling out of a hammock and topped up Miss Scrubshaw's glass while he began to explain the rules.

'Now,' he said. 'Take a good look at your hand.'

'Which one – the left or the right?' asked Mr Mate.

'I mean the hand of cards, you dozy dog,' glared the Captain.

The Captain's explanation of the rules went on for some time. Custardly didn't understand all of it. A pair, he gathered, was a good hand but it could be beaten by a run and a flush – which sounded like someone who urgently needed the toilet. Knaves or Jacks seemed to be the best cards and if you were lucky enough to have four Jacks that was a Parcel of Knaves, which couldn't be beaten.

Once the game began it was easy to tell who was winning by Miss Scrubshaw's shrieks of excitement. The Captain stroked his black beard and sank lower in his chair as the pile of money in front of him grew smaller and smaller. Mr Mate wasn't doing much better. Whenever a hand was dealt he would throw his cards down in disgust and then snatch them up again too late to prevent the others from seeing them. As

the game went on, Custardly noticed Miss Scrubshaw was behaving increasingly oddly. Her voice
grew louder and sometimes her words got muddled
up. If he didn't know better, Custardly might have
thought she was drunk.

'You know, Captain,' she said, waving her glass in
the air, 'this is very nice fruit pinch. I can't think why
I've never toasted it before.'

'Your deal, Constance,' said the Captain, passing
her the deck of cards. 'And by the by, your hair is
dangling in your drink.'

'Is it? How silly of me!' giggled Miss Scrubshaw,
fishing out a lock of hair and putting it in her mouth.
She leaned over the table, pointing a finger at the
Captain. 'Shall I tell you something, Captain? I'm
going to won all of your money – every last little
pinny.'

But as it turned out the Captain took the next
hand with a pair of aces and after that Miss Scrubshaw's luck seemed to desert her. The more she lost,
the more she bet and her pile of coins soon dwindled
to a small heap. At last, when the Captain laid down
a winning hand yet again, she slumped back in her
chair.

'That's the lot,' she declared miserably. 'I'm broke. Busted. Pennilessless.'

The Captain stroked his beard thoughtfully. 'Well, that's a pity, Constance,' he said. 'Because here I am with all this pile of money and no one to play. It don't seem fair not to give you the chance to win some of it back.'

'I'll take it off you,' offered Mr Mate. 'I haven't won a bean all night.'

The Captain ignored him and leaned forward over the table.

'Tell you what,' he said. 'What if we was to play one last hand, Constance? One last hand and I'll stake everything I've won tonight.'

Miss Scrubshaw widened her eyes. 'All of it?'

'All of it,' said the Captain, pushing the mountain of coins into the middle of the table.

'But I haven't got anything left to bet,' said Miss Scrubshaw.

The Captain's face took on a crafty look. 'Oh, I wouldn't say that. There must be something. What about that worthless old map your uncle left you?'

Miss Scrubshaw blinked. 'Uncle Mack's jap?'

'Uncle Jack's map,' nodded the Captain.

'That's what I said, only my words keep getting middled,' giggled Miss Scrubshaw.

The Captain tipped the bottle and shook the last few drops of grog into her glass.

'What do you say, Constance? One last hand and the winner takes all.'

'I don't know. You see, my ankle left me that map when he dieded.'

'Your uncle?'

'That's what I said. And I really couldn't bear to lose it,' said Miss Scrubshaw.

'Come now,' said the Captain. 'What's one worthless old map when you could buy a hundred just the same?'

He picked up a handful of coins and let them run through his fingers. Miss Scrubshaw watched with greedy eyes. Abruptly, she got to her feet and crossed to the study to unlock the door. A moment later she was back with the map and threw it on to the table.

The Captain licked his lips, shuffled the cards and began to deal two hands. Mr Mate, sulking because he was out of the game, lit his pipe and puffed out smoke.

Miss Scrubshaw picked up her cards and a smile

of triumph spread across her face. The Captain scratched his knee and his hand crept down to the top of his boot. From the landing above, the boys saw him slip an extra card into his hand.

'Did you see that? He's cheating!' whispered Dobbs.

'Of course he is – he's been cheating all along!' replied Custardly.

Miss Scrubshaw laid down her cards one by one. 'Three little kings,' she said. 'My money I think, Captain.' The Captain raised one eyebrow and spread his own cards on the table.

Mr Mate whistled low. 'Four Knaves! You have the luck of the devil, Captain.'

'Luck has nothing to do with it,' winked the Captain, rolling up the map and slipping it into his coat pocket. He scooped up the rest of his winnings and dropped the money into his purse. 'Well, it's been a real pleasure, Constance,' he said. 'We must do it again sometime. Oh, and by the by, I thought I might take the class on a little trip tomorrow.'

Miss Scrubshaw's head had drooped down towards the table. She raised it with an effort.

'A little drip?'

'Yes, to the sea. Do them good. Put some colour in their cheeks. I trust you don't have any objection?'

Miss Scrubshaw got to her feet rather unsteadily, leaning heavily on the back of a chair.

'I think, Captain, I will have to . . . oh dear!' She raised a hand to her head and swayed like a tree in the breeze. 'I think I will need to give that some therious short. No, I'm middling my words again. What I mean to say is . . .'

There was a loud thud as she let go of the chair, toppled sideways and hit the floor.

Peering down, Custardly could see her black boots sticking out from under the fallen chair. She seemed to be snoring loudly. The Captain stepped over her, his pockets jingling with coins.

'I'll take that as a yes then,' he said. His eyes travelled upwards to the banisters where two pale faces stared down at him. 'And as for you two young scoundrels, we've an early start in the morning so time you was both in bed.'

Custardly and Dobbs didn't need any more prompting. They sprang to their feet and hurried back to their dormitory before the Captain had a chance to come after them.

Chapter 5

The Salty Gherkin

The stagecoach pulled up outside a tavern called The Jolly Sailor and the children climbed down excitedly. It had been a long journey from Dankmarsh, especially with twenty children, two pirates and one very pale schoolteacher jammed into one coach. Custardly and his friends had been forced to squash on to the roof with the baggage, where they hung on for dear life as the stagecoach rattled and lurched around corners at

47

alarming speeds of up to twenty miles an hour.

'There she is, shipmates!' shouted Mr Mate.

At the foot of the hill they could see the harbour bristling with masts, yardarms and other boaty things. Custardly breathed in the sharp salty air and marvelled at the number of ships. He had never realised the sea was such a busy place. Miss Scrubshaw, meanwhile, climbed out of the coach in her crumpled bonnet, looking as green as a gooseberry.

She couldn't remember much of the night before

or how she had come to agree to this trip. All she knew was that her head felt like someone had been using it as a tambourine. If anyone mentioned grog, she was going to be very sick.

The Captain led the way along the bustling harbour until he came to a halt at an impressive ship with three tall masts and six cannons on either side.

'There she is – *The Salty Gherkin*,' he said proudly.

Custardly stared. 'Is she really yours?'

'Mine, shipmate, and you won't find a finer ship on the seven seas.'

Mr Mate coughed. 'Well, apart from *The Black Tadpole*, Captain. She's a lot faster. And *The Pelican* has more guns . . .' He tailed off, noticing the Captain grinding his teeth. 'I'll just see to the gangplank, shall I?' he said.

Miss Scrubshaw, who had been trailing some way behind, now pushed her way through the crowd of excited children. '*The Salty Gherkin*? What is the meaning of this, Captain?'

'Meaning?' said the Captain. 'Well, a gherkin is a kind of vegetable –'

'Not the name!' thundered Miss Scrubshaw. 'I mean, what are we doing here? You said nothing about setting foot on a boat. I do not like boats, Captain. Boats do not agree with me.'

'Now you come to mention it, you are looking a bit green at the gills,' said the Captain. 'We're going to take a little tour of the ship so why don't you slip into that tavern there and have a mug of sweet tea? We can look after the children for a bit, ain't that right, Mr Mate?'

'Aye, Captain,' replied the mate with a wink. 'We can look after 'em.'

Miss Scrubshaw didn't need much persuading. Right now she couldn't think of anything worse than clambering over a ship and feeling the deck moving beneath her feet. She brightened even more when the Captain offered to escort her to the tavern and pay the landlord to look after her. (He was a charming man with a black eyepatch.)

Meanwhile Mr Mate led the excited children up the gangplank to begin the tour.

Custardly had always dreamed of setting foot on board a real ship and *The Salty Gherkin* was everything he'd imagined. Mr Mate led them up and down narrow stairways, peeping into the galley, where dirty pots and pans lay in the sink and the

Captain's cabin, where a table was heaped with maps and charts. Finally the mate took them below to the gun deck where he said he had one or two jobs to do and left them to play by themselves.

Custardly found a pile of old cannonballs in a corner and they were soon enjoying a game of skittles across the deck. The game was just reaching an exciting point, with Custardly about to take his third shot, when the deck gave a violent lurch and he almost dropped the cannonball on his foot.

'What was that?' asked Dobbs.

'I don't know,' said Custardly. The escaped cannonball rolled across the deck by itself and came to rest in a corner. Dobbs went to one of the gunwhales and peered out.

'Hey, the dock is moving!' he cried.

The others crowded round to see for themselves.

'It's not the dock that's moving, it's us!' shouted Custardly.

They clattered upstairs to the deck, where they found Mr Mate at the wheel of the ship and the Captain bellowing out orders. 'Hoist the mizzen, Mr Mate! Weigh anchor! Hard down on your left as she goes!'

'Beg'n your pardon, Captain,' puffed the mate, 'but I can't be hoisting and hauling and steering at the same time – I've only got one pair of hands.'

The Captain caught sight of Custardly. 'You, shipmate!' he roared. 'Take the wheel! Keep her steady!'

Custardly did as he was told, mainly because the mate had let go of the wheel and the ship was in danger of scraping the harbour wall.

As *The Salty Gherkin* slipped past the harbour, the children crowded to the rails. A woman in a black bonnet was chasing along the dock, hitching up her skirts and shouting.

'STOP!' cried Miss Scrubshaw. 'Kidnapper! Thief! Turn that ship –'

Her next words were drowned out by a great splash as she reached the end of the dock and dropped like a stone into the water below. A moment later she bobbed up like a cork, spluttering and gasping for breath. 'Urgle flub! COME . . . glug! . . . BACK!'

Dobbs turned to Custardly, who was steering for the open sea.

'What did she say?' he asked.

'I'm not sure,' replied Custardly. 'But it sounded something like, "Go on without me."'

Chapter 6

Riddles!

*T*he *Salty Gherkin* bobbed along on a calm sea.
On deck, however, all was not well.

'It's not fair! You tricked us!' said Angela. 'You said
we were going on a trip but you just wanted to kid-
nap us.'

'Yes,' said Custardly. 'We've been talking it over
and we've decided to hold a mutey thing.'

'A mutiny,' prompted Dobbs.

'Yes, one of those.'

'Lads, lads, you've got this all wrong!' The Captain held up a hand for quiet. 'First off, I promised you a trip to the sea. Well, I'm a man of my word. This is a trip and ain't that the sea you're looking at?'

'Well, yes,' said Custardly, 'but –'

'And second, shipmates,' the Captain went on, 'let me ask you this – where would you rather be now? Back at school with old Miss Starchpants or on a ship with the breeze in your hair and the sun on your back?'

The children considered it. When you put it like that the Captain hadn't really kidnapped them at all, he'd actually helped them escape.

'And thirdly,' said the Captain, 'who has kidnapped who? You don't look like kids to me – you looks like a proper crew of pirates!'

'Do we?' asked Dobbs.

'Certainly,' said the Captain. 'And since you is pirates, it's high time you changed out of them lubberly clothes. Mr Mate!'

The mate pulled out an old sea chest and opened it to reveal it was stuffed full of shirts, spotted headscarves, belts, boots, daggers and cutlasses. The Captain left them to try on their new clothes and, having dealt with the mutiny, retired to his cabin for a well-earned nap.

Two hours later Custardly knocked on the cabin door.

'Enter!' bellowed a voice.

He found the Captain munching a Ginger Crunch and studying Miss Scrubshaw's old map.

'Ah! Just the lad I wanted to see!' he cried, looking up. 'Take a seat, shipmate, and help yourself to biscuits. What kind's your favourite?'

'Chocolate,' said Custardly.

'Mine too,' agreed the Captain. 'Have a Custard Cream. I never touch 'em.'

Custardly glanced round the cabin. It was cramped and untidy, with socks, papers and biscuit crumbs littering the floor. On the wall was a portrait of the Captain looking moodily out to sea with a telescope in his hand. Various ship's instruments were scattered round the room and there was a shelf of books with titles like *Navigation Made Easy*, *The Wicked Book of Sea Shanties* and *Eyepatches for All Occasions*.

'Now, shipmate,' said the Captain, 'cast your eye over this and tell me what you make of it.'

Custardly looked at the map spread out on the table. It showed an island, and scrawled across it in black ink was the name:

DOOM ISLAND

'Doom Island?' said Custardly. 'Is that where we're going?'

'Oh, don't let the name worry you,' said the Captain. 'That's just something we pirates call it for effect. Have another biscuit!'

Custardly helped himself. 'So it isn't dangerous or anything?' he said.

'Dangerous? Lord bless you, no!' laughed the Captain. 'There's nothing there but sand and sea. You might come across a sea turtle or a few parrots but nothing that would give you nightmares at all.' The Captain pulled a flask from his pocket and took a long swig of grog.

'And this is where you think the treasure is buried?' asked Custardly.

'Oh, it's there all right,' said the Captain. 'This is Black Jack Mulligan's map and everyone knows he was rich as the King of Spain. But that's the part that's got me foxed. See for yourself, lad – it don't make sense.'

Custardly studied the map in more detail. Apart from cheery names like Hangman's Hill and Coffin Cove, it seemed ordinary enough.

'It looks all right to me,' he said.

'All right?' repeated the Captain. 'Where's the X? How the devil do we find a treasure without an X marks the spot?'

Custardly ran his eye over the island again. 'What's this?' he asked, pointing to a dark splodge in the

hills. The Captain dabbed at it and licked his finger. 'Blackberry jam,' he said. 'Mulligan's favourite.'

Custardly took the map to the window where the evening sun was spilling into the cabin. When he held the paper up to the light, he immediately saw what they'd been missing. 'Look at this, Captain. There's something written on the back.'

The words were faint and scrawled in spidery black writing. Custardly read them out slowly.

Dark I am and cold as death.
Mouth I own but have no breath.
Speak to me, yourself replies.
In my heart the treasure lies.'

The Captain snatched the map and read the words several times, frowning hard. Finally he threw it down on the table in disgust.

'Mouth I own but have no breath? What kind of bilge is that? If Black Jack Mulligan wrote this, he'd drunk too much grog.'

'But don't you see?' said Custardly. 'It must be some sort of riddle.'

'Riddle?' frowned the Captain.

'You know, a riddle like ... "What do you call a cat with eight legs?"'

The Captain knitted his brows. 'A cat with eight legs? There's no such thing!'

'No, it's a sort of joke,' said Custardly. 'What do you call a cat with eight legs? An octo-puss!'

The Captain's puzzled face slowly broke into a great grin. 'AH-HAAAARR!' he roared, punching Custardly on the shoulder. 'An octopus! Wait till I tell Mr Mate that one. A cat with eight legs, an octopus! Har har har! An octopus!'

'Yes,' said Custardly, who felt a joke was never quite as funny when you kept repeating it. 'But the point is, it's some kind of clue. If we can solve the riddle, maybe it'll lead us to the treasure.'

The Captain pushed the biscuit barrel across the table. 'Smart thinking, shipmate. Have another. No, take a chocolate one. I insist.'

He began to pace the cabin excitedly. 'I knew you was a sharp one the first time I clapped eyes on you. So riddles, you say – riddles? And if we can find this eight-legged octopus it will lead us to the spot?'

'Um, no, forget the octopus,' said Custardly. 'Just let me take this away and try to work it out.'

He copied out the riddle on to a piece of paper and slipped it into his pocket. If anyone was able to solve the clues, it would be Dobbs, who was a genius at any kind of puzzle.

When it came to riddles, he had a feeling the Captain wasn't going to be much help.

Chapter 7

Doom Island

'LAND AHOY!' cried Rose from high in the crow's nest.

Everyone rushed to the ship's rail, eager to get their first glimpse of the island.

Doom Island certainly lived up to its name. Black rocks like giant's teeth guarded the coast. To the east were tall cliffs, to the west a wide beach backed by forest, and over it all a grey blanket of fog that looked as though it would never lift.

'Is that it? asked Dobbs with a shiver.

'Maybe it looks better on a sunny day,' said Custardly.

But it was hard to imagine the sun ever shining on Doom Island. There was no sign of the brightly coloured parrots that the Captain had talked about. Black shapes wheeled and dived from the cliffs but they didn't look like the kind of birds you'd keep as a pet.

The Captain meanwhile was busy giving orders. He announced that once they'd dropped anchor in the bay a landing party would go ashore. Immediately he was flattened in the stampede as the crew all rushed to be first in the boat.

'WAIT!' he roared. 'What the devil do you think you're doing?'

'Getting in the boat,' replied Angela. 'I want to be in the landing party.'

'Me too,' said Rose. 'Will there be jelly and cake?'

The Captain scowled. 'First of all, it ain't that kind of party. Secondly, it's my boat and I say who gets in. And thirdly . . . um, what is thirdly, Mr Mate?'

'The one after secondly, Captain,' said the mate helpfully.

'No, thirdly, someone has to stay on board and guard the ship.'

This was received with a good deal of grumbling.

'I'm bored of being on board,' complained Angela.

'Me too,' moaned Rose.

'And me,' added George. 'I want to go to the island and dig for treasure!'

Everyone started to talk at once but the Captain settled the argument by saying there would be an extra ration of biscuits for everyone who stayed behind. In the end it was decided the landing party would be made up of the Captain, Mr Mate, Custardly and Dobbs (the Captain because it was his boat and the others because he said so).

Later that afternoon they dragged their rowing boat ashore and beached it on the grey sand. Custardly walked a little way up the beach and bent to pick something up.

'Someone's been here before,' he said.

'Don't talk bilge,' scoffed the Captain. 'This island is deserted.'

'Then how do you explain this?' asked Custardly, holding up a soggy black sock.

'All kinds of things get washed up,' shrugged the Captain. Nevertheless, Custardly noticed he drew his cutlass and kept glancing about him as they went on.

'Stick together and follow me,' he said, bravely striding on ahead. He hadn't got far when he vanished from sight with a surprised yell.

The others rushed forward and found him lying face down at the bottom of a deep hole.

'Beg'n your pardon, Captain, but what are you doing down there?' asked Mr Mate.

'MMMNNNFFFGGGH!' replied the Captain through a mouthful of sand.

The mate shook his head. 'Looks to me like you fell in a hole.'

'You'll be in a hole if you don't pull me out!' threatened the Captain, scrambling to his feet.

'Wait a minute,' said Custardly. 'A hole doesn't just appear. How did it get here?'

'Well, obviously someone must have dug it,' replied Dobbs.

'Exactly,' said Custardly. 'And if someone dug it then that means –'

What it meant became clear as a wild rabble burst out of the trees and poured towards them, brandishing cutlasses and yelling like savages.

'RARRGGHHHHH!'

Mr Mate was so surprised he took a step backwards and fell into the hole, landing on top of the Captain. Dobbs and Custardly both tried to run but collided and tumbled in too. Once they had stopped struggling and had sorted out who was on top of who, they looked up to find seven ugly faces scowl-

ing down at them. Something about their ragged clothes, gold earrings and unshaven faces made Custardly suspect they were pirates.

'Well, well, if it ain't our old mate Captain Yellerbelly!' sneered the pirate with a gold tooth, who seemed to be the leader. The Captain settled his squashed hat back on his head and stood up.

'Sly Morgan, Runnynose Ralph and Neffy Norris,' he said. 'What a treat to see you boys again. I've been worried sick.'

Sly Morgan spat on the ground. 'Worried, eh? Strange, that, because you're the scurvy knave that took the ship and left us here to die.'

'Macarooned!' wailed Neffy Norris, startling a cloud of flies buzzing around him.

'Lads, lads!' said the Captain, sweating a little. 'You've got this all wrong. You don't think I'd abandon my own crew? Why do you think I've come back?'

Mr Mate tugged at his sleeve. 'Beg'n your pardon, Captain, but you said we was coming back for the treasure.'

'No I didn't,' said the Captain, glaring at him.

'Yes you did. 'Cos I said what about Sly and the others? And you said they're probably dead by now and who cares 'cos it's all the more treasure for us.'

An uncomfortable silence followed this speech. The pirate gang toyed with their cutlasses and fiddled with their pointy sticks. It was Custardly who spoke next.

'So hang on, you've been to this island before?'

'Well, I may have passed by,' admitted the Captain.

'Oh he knows this island all right,' said Sly Morgan. 'It was him persuaded us to come and look for Black Jack Mulligan's treasure. But there never was no gold, was there, Captain? Five days we searched this island from top to tail and we never found a farthing. We was all for giving up but the Captain says, "Just one more day, lads. One more day and our luck will turn." Well, our luck turned all right – the very next night that's when they came.'

'They?' said Custardly. 'Who?'

'Ah, so you ain't told them yet, Captain?' Sly Morgan smiled. 'Funny that should slip your mind.'

'Told us what?' asked Custardly. 'What are you talking about?'

Sly Morgan glanced at the sky and lowered his voice to a whisper. 'The flying fiends,' he said.

Custardly raised his eyebrows. Maybe these pirates had been on the island so long they were starting to imagine things.

'Oh, think I'm mad, do you?' said Morgan. 'Then ask the Captain. Ask him why he scarpered with the boat and left us to die.'

The pirates murmured darkly among themselves and closed in around the hole. Custardly had a feeling things were about to turn ugly.

'Well,' he said, 'It's been lovely chatting, but if you don't mind we really ought to be getting back to the ship.' He reached up a hand to the edge of the hole, but a heavy boot trod on his fingers.

'Not so fast – you ain't going nowhere,' sneered Sly Morgan. 'This time it'll be us taking the ship. You and your mates can stay here and keep the Captain company.'

Neffy Norris suddenly pointed past them, out to sea. 'The ship! She's shrinking!'

'She isn't shrinking,' said Runnynose Ralph, 'she's heading out to sea!'

They all turned to look at *The Salty Gherkin* which had left the bay and was now getting smaller and smaller.

'Mr Mate!' roared the Captain. 'Didn't I order you to drop anchor?'

'Of course, Captain,' said the mate. 'I dropped it downstairs where no one would trip over it.'

'You dozy barnacle! I meant drop it overboard!'

Custardly groaned. 'But if the ship's not anchored it could drift for miles! How are we going to get home?'

The pirates stared after *The Salty Gherkin* as it headed out to sea, sailing ever further from the island.

Neffy Norris sank to his knees. 'We're macarooned!' he wailed.

Chapter 8

A Bunch of Knots

The sun was sinking and so were Custardly's hopes of ever seeing his friends again. By now the ship might be miles away. As it grew darker, their captors seemed nervous and took them back to a ramshackle hut in the woods. It stank of dead fish, woodsmoke and Neffy Norris's smelly socks. Custardly watched Runnynose Ralph tying rope round Dobbs's ankles.

'You're not going to leave it like that, are you?' asked Dobbs.

'Like what?' sniffed Ralph.

'Like that. It's a granny knot. Even a five-year-old could untie it!'

Runnynose Ralph looked worried. 'You're not thinking of escaping, are you?' he growled. 'Only you'll get me in trouble.'

'That's why you should always use a reef knot,' said Dobbs.

'A whatnot?'

'No, a reef knot. It's what sailors use. They're impossible to untie.'

Ralph wiped his nose with his sleeve. 'I was never very good at knots.'

'Start again and I'll show you,' offered Dobbs. 'Now, take one end and make a loop . . .'

Custardly rolled his eyes. Here they were, prisoners of a cut-throat gang of pirates, and all Dobbs could think of was knot-tying lessons. He glanced around the hut. Two of the pirates leaned in the doorway while the others sat watching the sky through the windows. All of them seemed to be afraid of something. Just then Sly Morgan swept in

wearing the Captain's lace-trimmed hat.

'Avast there!' he cried, striking a captainly pose with his hands on his hips.

No one took much notice. Neffy Norris looked up. 'What about the prisoners, Sly?'

'Call me Captain! I told you before,' said Sly sulkily.

'Sorry, Captain, but what shall we do with 'em?'

'Put crabs down their trousers!' grinned Toothless Tim.

'Or sand in their boots!'

'Make them eat Neffy Norris's seaweed stew!' cried Runnynose Ralph.

'Quiet, you swabs!' roared Sly Morgan. 'I'm the Captain round here and I say what we do with 'em. It's going to be something so wicked and bad that only a captain could have thought of it.'

'What?' said the dim-witted pirates, crowding round eagerly.

Sly lowered his voice. 'All right, boys, I say we take 'em into the woods and leave 'em.'

The pirates nodded. 'Yes?'

'In the dark. By themselves. Without a lantern.'

'But Captain, if we leave them, won't they escape?' asked Runnynose Ralph.

'Curses!' muttered Sly. 'I never thought of that.'

The Captain, who had been listening closely to all this, shook with laughter.

'And what's so funny?' growled Sly, turning on him.

'You, Sly Morgan. Thinking that wearing my hat makes you a captain.'

Sly Morgan glared furiously. 'I'm more of a captain than you are! You couldn't captain . . . a carrot.'

'Oh no? Well, you couldn't captain a cabbage!' the Captain shot back.

'And you couldn't captain a plate of peas!'

75

This exchange of vegetables could have gone on for some time but the Captain changed tack. 'Well, if you're so clever, why ain't you found Mulligan's treasure?' he taunted. 'You've had long enough to look for it.'

Sly Morgan glowered. 'There never was no treasure and you know it.'

'Is that so?' The Captain caught Custardly's eye and gave him a wink. 'Then what if I was to tell you that Black Jack Mulligan left *a treasure map*?'

This got the pirates' attention and they gathered round, their eyes shining with greed.

'A treasure map?'

'Where?'

'Pay no attention. He's lying,' growled Sly Morgan.

The Captain shrugged. 'You're the captain. I'm sure you know best, shipmate.' He hummed a sea shanty to himself.

This only enraged Sly Morgan all the more and he whipped out a dagger from his belt. 'Show us then! If you've got Mulligan's map, let's see it!'

The Captain laughed. 'Oho! You don't think I'm fool enough to carry it around?'

Mr Mate looked up. 'Captain . . .'

'It's back on the ship,' said the Captain, ignoring him. 'I left it in my cabin.'

'Well, what use is that? The ship is gone!' cried Sly Morgan.

The Captain shuffled a little closer on his bottom. 'But think, shipmate, maybe it ain't too late. If we was to go after them in the boat, we might still catch 'em. Bring me to the ship and the map is yours, pirate's honour.'

'He's right,' said Runnynose Ralph. 'Maybe it's not too late.'

'But Captain . . .' interrupted Mr Mate.

'I don't know,' said Sly Morgan. 'This sounds like a scurvy trick to me. How do I know you won't double-cross me once we reach the ship? Maybe you've got men on board waiting to spring an ambush.'

The Captain, who had been thinking exactly that, pretended to look hurt. 'Shipmate! When did I ever tell you a lie?'

'But Captain, listen!' Mr Mate finally butted in. 'We don't need the ship because the map's in your pocket. I saw you put it there!'

Sly Morgan laughed, showing his gold tooth. 'Ahaar! So who's clever now? Search his pockets, boys!'

The Captain glared at his mate. 'You dozy dog! Why can't you keep your big mouth shut?'

It didn't take long for the pirates to find the map. Sly Morgan seized it and spread it out on a wooden box in the glow of a lantern. The rest of the pirates crowded round, pushing and shoving to get a better look. For a minute Morgan studied the map in silence, frowning at the words he couldn't read, then he brought his fist down with a thump.

'What kind of map do you call this?' he roared. 'Where's the X marks the spot?'

The Captain shrugged. 'Search me, mate. You're the clever one – you work it out.'

Custardly smiled to himself. Even if the pirates found the riddle on the back, they didn't have the brains to solve it. Dobbs had been struggling for the past two days to make sense of the clues. He watched Neffy Norris and Ralph fight over the map which was in danger of being torn to pieces.

Sly Morgan suddenly raised a hand in the air and shouted above the noise.

'Silence you swabs! LISTEN!'

Everyone stopped shouting and listened. Custardly noticed many of the pirates had turned deathly pale. Then he heard it – a drumming, whirring noise filling the air like a whirlwind approaching.

'It's them!' gasped Neffy Norris. 'They're coming!'

'The fiends!' whimpered Runnynose Ralph.

'Courage, lads! Stand by your posts!' trembled Sly Morgan, snuffing out the light. But the terrified pirates weren't standing at all. They had dived under beds and blankets or anything they could find, where they lay quivering like jellies. The only two left sitting upright were Custardly and Dobbs. The noise in their ears grew louder and louder . . .

Chapter 9

Attack!

A moment later it sounded like large hailstones were thudding off the roof of the hut. Through the window Custardly glimpsed black shapes as big as buzzards swooping and diving, trying to find a way in. The Captain was huddled in a corner with Mr Mate on his lap, whimpering like a baby. Custardly shuffled under a table, where he found Dobbs had already taken refuge. They had to shout to make themselves heard above the din.

'What are they?' yelled Custardly.

'Bats!'

'They're monsters!'

'Hamsters?'

'No, I said . . . never mind!'

At that moment one of the giant bats came crashing through the roof in a flurry of sticks and leaves. It plummeted towards the ground then righted itself with a flap of its wings. Custardly saw its cruel black eyes and squashed, ugly face as it flapped wildly through the hut, seeking a victim.

Sly Morgan lost his nerve and broke from his hiding place. In an instant the bat swooped after him. For a moment it looked as if it might carry him off, then he struck out with his sword and the thing was out through the door, sweeping off into the night.

The beating of wings gradually died away and all was quiet.

Very slowly the pirates crept out of their hiding places, looking pale and shaken.

'Yikes!' said Custardly. 'What was THAT?'

'The fiends,' said Runnynose Ralph. 'Every night they come. Three months ago they took Seasick Sid.

We never seen him again.'

'But what are they?' asked Custardly.

'Bats, I told you,' said Dobbs.

The Captain shook his head. 'I never seen bats the size of that.'

'That's not surprising,' said Dobbs. 'From what I saw they're a very rare species. *Desmodus humongous.*'

'And what's that if you don't speak French?' asked the Captain.

'It means Giant Vampire Bat.'

'Vampires?' Custardly gulped. 'You mean they actually drink blood?'

'Oh yes,' said Dobbs. 'It's what they live on. Cow's blood, sheep's blood – they drink anything they can find.'

'But not, you know . . . human blood?' said Custardly.

Dobbs shrugged. 'Actually, I don't think they're too fussy.'

Late into the night, Sly Morgan and his gang sat up poring over Mulligan's map and arguing over how the treasure should be divided. Sly claimed that as captain he had a right to a bigger slice of the cake than anyone else. Runnynose Ralph grumbled that if there was any cake it ought to be shared equally. Neffy Norris said that he liked chocolate cake best. Toothless Tim worried that if the cake had been buried for years it might have gone stale. The argument went on while the pirates passed round the flask of grog they'd found in the Captain's pocket. At long last they crawled under their blankets and fell asleep one by one.

The Captain shuffled over to the others on his bottom. 'Shipmates!' he hissed. 'Now's our chance to escape!'

Custardly gave him a look. 'How can we when we're tied up?'

'We can hop!' said the Captain. 'Follow me!'

He struggled to his feet and hopped towards the door. Hopping with both feet tied together isn't easy at any time but hopping with your hands tied behind your back makes it almost impossible. The Captain wobbled, tripped over Mr Mate's legs and collapsed in a heap.

Over by the door, Sly Morgan stirred in his sleep and clutched the treasure map to his chest.

'This is hopeless!' groaned Custardly.

'Wouldn't it be easier if someone untied us?' whispered Dobbs.

'Oh, good idea!' said Custardly sarcastically. 'And who's going to do that?'

Dobbs did something behind his back that involved a lot of wriggling around and pulling faces. When he brought out his hands he was holding a piece of rope and looking pleased with himself.

'Wow!' said Custardly, impressed. 'Where did you learn that?'

Dobbs shrugged. 'Reef knots are easy peasy.'

'I thought you said they were impossible to untie.'

'Yes, sorry, I sort of lied about that,' admitted Dobbs. 'The reef knot's fine if you just want to fasten a sail but if you want something stronger –'

'Dobbs,' interrupted Custardly.

'What?'

'Maybe we could talk about knots *after* we've escaped?'

'Oh, OK. Just let me untie my feet,' said Dobbs.

Ten minutes later the four of them emerged on to the beach, panting for breath. The Captain had rescued his hat while the mate held a lantern he'd stolen to light their way.

'This way,' pointed Custardly. He remembered they'd hidden the rowing boat among the rocks.

The Captain grabbed him by the arm. 'Hold fast there, shipmate. Ain't you forgetting what we came for?'

Custardly groaned. 'You're not still thinking about the treasure?'

'Why not? If we leave now we may never get another chance.'

'But it's the middle of the night and, besides, we don't have the map,' argued Custardly.

The Captain grinned and pulled off his hat. He shook out a folded piece of paper.

'You don't think I'd let a weasel like Sly Morgan keep it, do you?'

Dobbs was watching the night sky nervously. 'What about the bats?' he asked. 'What if they come back?'

'Come now, lads, surely you ain't going to let a few little bats frighten you off?'

Custardly finally lost his patience. 'Firstly,' he said, 'we're not dealing with "a few little bats". And secondly, if you were listening, they are vampire bats – which means *they drink your blood*. If you ask me we should get away from this island while we can.'

He marched off towards the boat with the Captain hurrying after him.

'All right, shipmate, let's not be hasty. Fair's fair now, what do you say we take a vote?'

Custardly halted and turned round. 'Fine with me.'

'Right then,' said the Captain. 'All those in favour of cutting and running, raise your hand.'

Custardly and Dobbs both put up their hands.

'All those in favour of finding the treasure?'

The Captain raised his own hand and looked daggers at Mr Mate, who reluctantly joined him.

'Two against two,' said the Captain. 'But luckily there's a way to decide.'

'Oh, and what's that?' asked Custardly.

'Ship's rules, the captain always gets the casting vote.'

'That's not fair!' cried Dobbs. 'You're the captain.'

'Well, so I am,' winked the Captain. 'And I votes we find the treasure. This way, me hearties!'

Chapter 10

X Marks the Spot

An hour later they came out on top of Hangman's Hill. Below them the island and the ghostly sea were spread out in the moonlight. They had waded through rivers, squelched through swamps and trudged for miles along the sand, yet they were still no closer to finding Mulligan's treasure.

'Read it again,' ordered the Captain.

Custardly sighed. 'We've been over it a hundred times!'

'Again!' roared the Captain.

Custardly repeated the riddle which by now he knew off by heart.

> *Dark I be and cold as death.*
> *Mouth I own but have no breath.*
> *Speak to me, yourself replies.*
> *In my heart the treasure lies.'*

The Captain pulled at his beard irritably. 'Blast me breeches, it don't make no sense! What kind of thing has a mouth but no breath?'

Mr Mate frowned. 'Maybe it's you, Captain.'

'Me?'

'You're dark and you've got a mouth. A pretty big one, I'd say.'

The Captain scowled. 'If you don't pipe down, the treasure won't be all that's buried on this island.'

Mr Mate fell silent. Custardly studied the map in the dim glow of the lantern while Dobbs sat on a rock, staring out to sea. Suddenly he leapt up.

'That's it! When do you reply to yourself?'

'When you're mad as a mongoose,' replied the Captain.

'No,' said Dobbs. 'When you're an echo. "Speak to me, yourself replies."'

'Yes, that makes sense,' said Custardly. 'But what about the rest? And where are we going to find an echo?'

'In a church?' suggested the Captain.

'In your ears,' said Mr Mate.

'No! In a cave – look!' Dobbs pointed excitedly at the cliffs below where a cave led deep under the rock.

'"Dark I be and cold as death. Mouth I own but

have no breath." A cave is dark and cold and it has a mouth too. That's the answer!'

The Captain clapped Dobbs so hard on the back that his glasses almost flew off.

'Bless me, you're right, shipmate! It was staring us in the face the whole time. Come on – the treasure is as good as ours.'

'Wait,' said Custardly. 'Before we all rush down there, what are they?'

He pointed to the cliffs where black shapes flitted in and out of the moonlight. The Captain drew out his telescope and raised it to his eye. 'Seagulls,' he grunted.

Custardly shook his head. 'Those aren't seagulls. Think about it. What lives in caves and comes out at night?'

Custardly's teeth chattered. He was up to his knees in icy water, wading against a swirling current. Right now he would have given anything to be back in the classroom at Dankmarsh, listening to Miss Scrubshaw.

'Custardly,' said Dobbs, touching his arm, 'I'm scared.'

'Me too,' said Custardly. 'But they're only bats. I mean, what's the worst they can do? Suck out all your blood?'

'Right,' said Dobbs. 'Though strictly speaking they don't.'

'What?'

'Suck your blood. What they do is bite into your flesh and make two little holes. Then they kind of lap at your blood with their tongue, a bit like a kitten.'

'Thanks,' said Custardly. 'That makes me feel a lot better.'

Dobbs shrugged. 'You wanted to know.'

As they neared the cave, the water became more shallow. Custardly waved to the Captain and Mr Mate to hurry up. They were still struggling across the channel with the lantern held high and their swords between their teeth. Custardly peered into the mouth of the cave and was hit by a sulphurous stench like rotten eggs.

'Bat droppings,' said Dobbs, sniffing the air.

'Great,' said Custardly. 'I've always wanted to die up to my neck in bat poo.'

The Captain arrived. 'Courage, lads,' he urged. 'Just

think, somewhere in there is Black Jack Mulligan's treasure. Riches beyond your dreams. Right then, who's going first?'

Nobody moved. They listened to the wind moan and the steady drip, drip of water coming from the cave. Custardly hoped that the bats had fed well that night and were now sleeping soundly.

'So,' he said, 'I'm hoping you've got some kind of plan.'

'Of course,' said the Captain. 'Here's what we do, lads: creep in quiet as mice, grab the treasure and run like the blazes.'

'That's the plan?' said Custardly.

'In a nutshell.'

'Brilliant. And what if the bats aren't asleep? What if they see us?'

'They won't!' scoffed the Captain. 'Everyone knows bats are blind as bats.'

'Actually, that's not quite true,' said Dobbs. 'They can probably see in the dark better than us but it's not their eyesight you need to worry about. Bats have amazingly sharp ears – they can hear a flea scratching itself.'

'That settles it! Let's go back,' said Custardly.

'Stop worrying,' said the Captain. 'I told you, we won't make a sound.'

'We'd better not,' said Dobbs. 'Once we're inside don't speak or whisper or even breathe.'

'One question,' said Mr Mate. 'Is it OK if I whistle?'

The cave was darker than the inside of a dragon's belly. Mr Mate went first with the lantern. Next came Custardly, Dobbs and finally the Captain, who bravely volunteered to bring up the rear.

Custardly felt his way along the damp, clammy passage. The stench was so bad he had to hold his nose in case he passed out. Every now and then he stumbled on the bones of some dead creature or stepped in yet another sticky pile of bat poo.

A little way in, the passage narrowed to a gap no wider than a person and they squeezed through one at a time. The cave led on, deeper under the cliffs, growing colder all the time. With every step Custardly grew more convinced that this was a BAD IDEA and they ought to turn back. At last the passage led down into a cavernous chamber as big and gloomy as the dining room at Dankmarsh.

Custardly blinked, wondering if his eyes were playing tricks on him. In the middle of the cavern was an open wooden chest, set on a flat rock. It was full to the brim with gold, pieces of eight and precious stones of every kind. There were rubies, emeralds, opals and strings of fat pearls.

'Blister me bunions! Feast your eyes on that!' cried the Captain, forgetting to keep quiet. The booming echo of his voice was followed by a noise like the rustling of a thousand leaves. Custardly slowly raised his eyes and saw something that chilled him to the bone. The roof of the cave was alive with bats. Giant bats stared back at him, old bats twitched, young bats hung upside down by one foot, showing off.

'Steady lads – I don't think they've seen us,' whispered the Captain. 'Cover me and get ready to run.'

He took one step towards the treasure, but as he did so, something else moved. A huge brown pod on the roof began to unfold, revealing that it wasn't a pod at all but a bat so monstrous it made the others look like fruit flies. This could only be the king bat, and it hopped – or rather flopped – down from the ceiling and tottered towards them on its little clawed feet.

'Good evening,' it said, in a voice surprisingly deep
for a bat. Custardly gaped, though whether he was
more shocked by the bat's size or by hearing it speak
he didn't know.

The bat bared its yellow fangs in something resem-
bling a smile. 'How kind of you to join us.'

Custardly backed away. 'We're not . . . we can't. I mean, we didn't mean to wake you up.'

'Oh please, no apology necessary,' said King Bat. 'I always have a snack about this time of night. Human blood is my favourite, far tastier than a mouse's or rat's. Rat's blood is so thin, don't you find?'

Custardly could hear a horrible slopping sound coming from the creature's bulging belly. He couldn't help wondering if a diet of human blood had started to have a peculiar effect on the bat's behaviour. Not only was it talking, it was oddly dressed for a bat. A red headscarf hung from one ear while a glittering diamond brooch was pinned to its chest like a medal. Propped against the far wall was the scarf's previous owner – a grinning skeleton wearing a pair of boots.

Mr Mate pointed a trembling finger. 'Seasick Sid,' he moaned. 'I'd know them boots anywhere – he got them for his birthday.'

They had backed away until they were up against a wall and now there was nowhere to go. The bat cast a hungry eye over them. 'Now, who shall we have for starters? You perhaps?'

It made a sudden leap towards Dobbs, who was frozen with terror. Without stopping to think, Custardly stepped between them. He had some brave idea of drawing his sword but he'd forgotten that he no longer had one. (Sly Morgan had seen to that.)

The next moment he found himself pinned to the floor by a sharp claw pressing into his neck. King Bat bared his needle-sharp teeth.

'You're quite big for a bat, aren't you?' gasped Custardly, struggling to breathe.

'What did you say?' The claw relaxed and Custardly squirmed out from underneath.

'I'm just very impressed,' he said. 'I mean most bats I've seen are, well, like sparrows compared to you. I was wondering – would you say you're the biggest bat in the world?'

King Bat swelled out his chest so they could admire his diamond brooch.

'You know how much blood I drink every night?' he asked. 'Go on take a guess.'

'I don't know – half a pint?'

'Six,' said the bat. 'Six pints of blood every night.'

'Amazing!' marvelled Custardly.

'That's how I grew this big,' boasted the bat. 'Once I was a weakling like them.' He rolled his eyes to indicate the bats on the roof. 'Of course these days it's mostly rats and birds. I have my servants bring them.'

'So you never actually go out then?' asked Custardly.

King Bat stared at him. 'Why should I?'

'Oh, no reason. I just wondered if you missed it. You know – hunting for your own supper, the thrill of the chase . . .'

King Bat brought his face so close that Custardly could smell the creature's rancid breath. 'It's *the blood* I look forward to,' he breathed. 'Now let's get on, shall we? All this talking is making me hungry.'

Custardly gasped as a claw ripped open his shirt. He would have to talk fast. 'Only, with all this hanging around indoors,' he gabbled, 'maybe you're not as quick as you were.'

There was a heavy silence. King Bat narrowed his eyes. 'Are you saying I'm OVERWEIGHT?'

'No, no, of course not,' replied Custardly. 'Just maybe a little slower. Take the Amazonian Fruit Bat, for instance. How fast can that fly?'

Dobbs realised Custardly was looking at him. 'Oh, um . . . fast,' he stammered. 'Maybe forty miles an hour.'

'Call that fast?' sneered King Bat. 'Take a look at this.'

He drew himself up and shook out his great, black wings to their full span. Custardly gulped. It was like facing a dragon – a dragon with squirrel ears and vampire teeth.

'Even so,' he went on, 'if you were to give me a head start, I bet you'd never catch me.'

King Bat rocked from side to side, making a clicking noise in his throat which Custardly eventually realised was bat laughter.

'You? A miserable creature with stumps for wings!'

'They're called arms,' said Custardly. 'But I can run. I'm the fastest in my class.'

'Second fastest,' Dobbs whispered in his ear.

'You wouldn't make it as far as the passage,' sneered King Bat.

'I wouldn't be so sure,' said Custardly. 'You're out of practice.'

'Ha! Want to try me? Any time you like.'

'All right, but you have to give me a sporting chance,' said Custardly. 'Hide your eyes and count to, say, twenty.'

'Like this?' King Bat folded its wings round its body, tucking its head out of sight. 'One,' he said in a muffled voice. 'Two . . .'

Custardly turned to the others, who were still pressed against the wall and seemed to have lost the use of their legs.

'*Run!*' he mouthed silently.

They all ran for their lives – except the Captain, who dashed over to the treasure chest and began to stuff his pockets with gold and jewels. Mr Mate doubled back to grab him by the arm.

As they fled from the cavern, Custardly could feel a hundred pairs of eyes watching them from the roof. He could only hope the bats were as brainless as their master. They reached the passage and plunged into the darkness. There was a crash of breaking glass as Mr Mate dropped the lantern. Custardly blundered on, his heart thumping and his feet slipping and sliding in piles of bat poo. He scraped his elbows and knees as he ran blindly into walls and changed direction.

Back in his great hall, King Bat was still counting.

'Eight . . . nine . . . TWENTY! COMING!'

He stretched out his massive wings and swept into the air like a black vulture. A moment later the cavern echoed to a sound like thunder as a hundred giant bats took off and swooped after him.

Down the passage, Custardly heard them coming and knew time was running out. Their only chance was to reach the mouth of the cave and pray that his idea worked.

'Hurry!' he panted.

'I am hurrying!' gasped Dobbs.

They rounded a bend and a glimmer of light told Custardly it wasn't far. Seconds later he reached the spot where the passage narrowed to the entrance. He squeezed through the gap and reached out a hand to pull Dobbs after him.

Looking back, he could see the shapes of the two red-faced pirates puffing after them. Behind them and closing fast was the colossal shadow of King Bat. The Captain made it to the gap and shot through like an express train. But Mr Mate was slowing down and looked back just in time to see the monster bat swoop towards him, its wing-tips grazing the walls.

Seconds later, Custardly saw its eyes bulge with fear as three things became clear:

1. It had grown way too fat to fit through its own front door.
2. It was too late to stop.
3. It was about to . . .

WHUMP!

A single crack spread its way across the cave roof, followed by several bigger cracks and small flakes of rock coming loose. The squadron of bats just had time to wonder why the walls were spattered with blood and where that rumbling noise was coming from. Then the roof fell in on them with a deafening crash.

Chapter 11

Flying Biscuits

When the huge cloud of dust had finally settled Custardly looked round. Dawn was breaking and the sky was a rosy pink.

'Is everyone all right?' he asked.

The Captain got to his feet and dusted off his hat.

'Right as rain,' he said. 'Anyone seen Mr Mate?'

Mr Mate sat up and spat out a mouthful of pebbles. He looked like a marble statue caked in dust and bat poo.

Dobbs took off his glasses and wiped them with a hanky.

'That was amazing!' he said. 'How did you know it would work?'

'I didn't,' admitted Custardly. 'I remembered the cave got pretty narrow, so I took a chance old Blubber Belly wouldn't be able to follow us. He may have been big, but he had the brain of a woodlouse.'

The Captain wrapped an arm round Custardly's shoulders. 'Smart thinking, shipmate,' he said. 'I was about to slice off his head with my cutlass, but I didn't want to steal your thunder.'

Dobbs glanced back at the remains of the cave. The passage they'd escaped from was buried under a mound of rubble. Not everything had been destroyed however. King Bat's cavern had largely survived the rockfall and it now stood open to the wind. Mr Mate picked his way over a mountain of rocks to reach it.

'Pity about the treasure though,' said Dobbs. 'Now no one will ever find it.'

'Maybe they will, shipmates! Look here!' cried the voice of Mr Mate. They hurried over to find him scrabbling on his hands and knees. He had uncovered a brass handle. They cleared away the rubble, pulled hard and, slowly, out came the treasure chest. The Captain used his dagger to prise open the lid.

'We did it, shipmates. We're rich! Rich!' he cried, plunging his hands into shining piles of gold and jewels.

'Well, well! Sorry to spoil the party,' sneered a voice behind them.

They spun round to see Sly Morgan and the rest of his scurvy crew. They were armed with cutlasses and pointy sticks. It was Neffy Norris who had found the

telltale footprints in the sand which eventually led them to the cave.

The Captain stepped out to meet them. 'Now there's a lucky thing, lads! We was just on our way to find you!'

'Were you now?' said Sly Morgan, unable to take his eyes off the treasure.

'Well, you don't think we was planning to keep all the loot to ourselves, do you? Fair's fair, boys – you helped look for it so we'll split it between us. Half to me and a quarter each to you. What do you say?'

Sly Morgan plucked off the Captain's hat and set it on his own head.

'I'll tell you what,' he said, 'I've got a better idea. Why don't *we* keep the treasure and bury you under them rocks? That way everyone's happy.'

'Actually,' said Custardly, 'we'd be dead.'

Morgan pulled a dagger from his belt. 'And as you're the clever one, you can be first.'

Things might have gone very badly at this point if a loud boom hadn't suddenly split the air, followed by something whistling overhead.

'The ship!' shouted Mr Mate, pointing over Custardly's shoulder. 'We're saved!'

The Salty Gherkin had returned in the nick of time. As Angela would proudly explain later, they had been sailing in circles since yesterday afternoon blown back and forth at the mercy of the wind. Finally Angela and her crew had worked out how to trim the sails and steer the ship. They'd arrived back at the island just in time to hear the loud boom as the cave collapsed. Angela had steered for the bay and scanned the beach with her telescope. Seeing her friends were in trouble, she'd ordered the cannons to open fire with the only ammunition they could find – broken biscuits.

BOOM! A volley of Gingernuts whistled through the air and stung Sly Morgan on the ear.

'We're under attack!' he cried. 'Take cover!'

Morgan's cowardly crew scattered in all directions, looking for somewhere to hide.

Custardly and Dobbs took cover behind the treasure chest, where they found the Captain guarding it with both fingers in his ears.

BOOM! A hail of Custard Creams rained down on Runnynose Ralph, splatting him with yellow goo. Neffy Norris tried to run but the next salvo peppered his backside with biscuits. 'I've been macarooned!' he yelped, which for once was true.

Custardly and Dobbs sprang up and joined in the

attack, pelting their enemies with handfuls of rubies, emeralds and diamonds as big as duck eggs. Caught between the fire of the cannons and a barrage of precious stones, the pirates fled and hid behind the biggest rock they could find. A moment later a greyish flag emerged and waved in the air. (It looked suspiciously like a pair of old pants.)

'Mercy!' begged the pirates. 'We surrender!'

The Captain bravely came out from his hiding place and held up a hand.

'All right, lads – cease fire! The battle's over!' he bellowed.

BOOM! A hail of butter shortbread rained down on him like bullets.

Chapter 12

Shipmates All

That evening the crew of *The Salty Gherkin* crammed into the Captain's cabin for a mighty feast. Everyone was there except Sly Morgan and his scurvy gang, who had been set adrift in a rowing boat and left to find their way home.

The Captain had broken open his secret supply of biscuits — the double chocolate ones he kept hidden under his bed. At the height of the feast he stood up to make a short speech.

'Boil me bedsocks, shipmates!' he grinned. 'Didn't I promise you that I'd find the treasure?'

'Yes,' replied Custardly. 'Although it is Dobbs who deserves the credit. He's the one who solved the riddle.'

Dobbs blushed modestly as everyone cheered and thumped him on the back.

'And if it wasn't for Custardly,' he said, 'I wouldn't be alive. None of us would. He's the bravest of us all.'

'Right enough,' agreed the Captain. 'I knew that boy was a pirate from the moment I clapped eyes on him. Shipmate, come over here.'

Custardly rose to his feet and came round the table. The Captain produced a large feathered hat which he'd been keeping for special occasions and set it on Custardly's head.

'There,' he said. 'Now you looks like a proper pirate.' He drew out his cutlass. 'As Captain of this ship, I hereby name you First Officer of *The Salty Gherkin* and Keeper of the Ship's Biscuits.'

Custardly stood on a chair and swept off his hat with a flourish as his classmates cheered.

'But what about the rest of us?' It was Angela who

spoke up. 'Now we've found the treasure, do we have to go back to school ?'

A silence fell. The prospect of returning to Dank-marsh and Miss Scrubshaw's dreary lessons after all their adventures filled them with gloom.

'But listen,' said Custardly. 'Who knows where we are?'

'I do,' answered Mr Mate. 'We're somewhere in the south sea.'

'No,' said Custardly. 'I mean who knows we're here? Miss Scrubshaw doesn't, so how can she make us go back? I say we take a vote on it. All those in favour of going back to school say "Aye."'

No one spoke.

'All those in favour of living the life of a pirate, say "Aharrrr!"'

'AHARRRR!' cried everyone, pulling fierce piratical faces and waving their fists.

'Carried!' cried Custardly. 'Captain, what's our course?'

The Captain tugged at his black beard. 'That's a good question. Now you come to mention it, who's steering the ship?'

There was a shuddering crunch followed by a longer scraping noise. Everyone fell over and slid to one end of the cabin as *The Salty Gherkin* hit a sandbank and ran aground.

'Barnacles!' muttered the Captain.